How to Be Nice ...
and Other Lessons
I Didn't Learn

by Lynea R‌

Illustrated b

For my uncle, Al Lombino,
with love—for his humor, his optimism,
and his courage—L.B.

For Jackie—L.G.

For information contact:
MONDO Publishing
980 Avenue of the Americas
New York, NY 10018

Visit our web site at http://www.mondopub.com

Printed in USA

07 08 09 10 11   9 8 7 6 5 4 3 2 1

1-59336-726-0

Designed by E. Friedman

Library of Congress Cataloging-in-Publication Data
Bowdish, Lynea.
How to be nice-- and other lessons I didn't learn / by Lynea Bowdish ;
illustrated by Les Gray.
p. cm.
Summary: To fit in with her new stepfamily, fourth-grader Rosie tries to
become a nicer person, but when her good deeds backfire, she decides to just
be herself.
ISBN 1-59336-726-0 (pbk.)
[1. Stepfamilies--Fiction. 2. Helpfulness--Fiction. 3. Behavior--Fiction.]
I. Gray, Les, ill. II. Title.
PZ7.B67194How 2006
[Fic]--dc22
2005023100

CONTENTS

Chapter 1   The Problem With Nice   5

Chapter 2   An Itchy Outcome   11

Chapter 3   So Much for Being Neighborly   16

Chapter 4   Laundry Disaster   22

Chapter 5   A Plucky Problem   27

Chapter 6   Rosie Foster Doesn't Run From
             Trouble   33

Chapter 7   Keyboard Malfunction   38

Chapter 8   Rosie to the Rescue   43

CHAPTER ONE
THE PROBLEM WITH NICE

Maybe Kyla's problem is that she's from Ohio. I've never been anyplace other than New Jersey. That's where I live. I don't count the time I went to Philadelphia on a class trip. I threw up a lot that day and didn't get to see anything. But that's another story.

Kyla is my stepsister—my *new* stepsister, I should say. Her brother Timmy is three. Her mother Joellen and Pops were married two months ago. Then my new stepfamily (ugh) moved in with us. That was the end of my life as I knew it.

The problem is that they're *too* nice. Maybe all people from Ohio are that nice. Maybe that's why Ohio is where it is, out in the middle of the country. Maybe all the nice people in the United States reside there. That way they only have to put up with each other.

My name is Rosie Foster. Rosie's short for Rosalind, but only Pops knows that. I swore him to secrecy a long time ago. My mother loved the playwright Shakespeare, so I got stuck with a name from one of his plays. If my mother had lived past my first birthday, I might have convinced her to change it. But she died. The first thing I said when I started to talk was that my name was Rosie.

Sometimes Pops calls me Stubby. That's another thing that's just between us. I'm short. A little chunky. A little, well, stubby.

Kyla, in addition to being nice, is the exact opposite. Of course. She's tall. Okay, she's a year older than me—she's going into the fifth grade—but she's still tall. And graceful, too. Her long hair is the color of dark chocolate, and her eyes match perfectly.

I wouldn't care if her only fault was being pretty, but her being super nice was just too much. It put me over the edge.

I tried to explain it to Pops. "She's nice," I said. It was the first time I'd gotten him alone in two months, and that was only because my new step-family was in Ohio visiting relatives.

"I'm glad you like her," Pops mumbled. He was grading history papers; he teaches summer school at a local college. The rest of the year, he teaches at a private high school.

"No, I mean she's *too* nice," I explained. I put a lot of emphasis on the "too."

He looked up. "You mean she's phony? I don't think she's phony."

"That's the problem," I said. "She's not phony at all. She's genuinely nice. I mean, she actually means what she says."

"What's wrong with that?" asked Pops. Now I had his undivided attention.

"She'll never survive here," I insisted. "The kids at school—they won't get her. Like, when I say something sarcastic, she just smiles. Joellen's the same way. She smiles at me constantly. And she makes oatmeal cookies just because she knows I like them."

"So?" Pops asked.

"Kyla offered to share a bedroom with Timmy, so I could go on having my own room," I said, amazed. "Do you realize how weird that is? And she told me that when school starts next month, I shouldn't feel like I have to hang out with her."

"She sounds thoughtful," Pops answered, sounding perplexed. "I don't know what your problem is."

"It's just not normal," I insisted. "Besides, I'm not used to nice." I said. "It would be a lot easier if she were nasty. Then I could hate her."

"Sorry, Stubby. Deal with it," Pops said. He went back to his papers.

Okay, I thought. *I'll deal with it.* If nothing else, I figured I could hate her just for being nice. Why do I want to hate her, you ask? That's easy. With her being so nice, everyone is sure to like her more than me. Obviously, Joellen does. After all, she's her mother. And Timmy does too, of course. But the person I'm mainly concerned about is Pops.

Pops thinks Kyla's perfect. That's because she's fascinated by the Civil War—my father's specialty. Kyla knows dates, battles, and why the war was fought, and she and Pops have actual conversations about it.

The following week, I found out that even Carmen liked Kyla. Carmen is my best friend. Kyla offered to lend Carmen a shirt that she had admired.

"Really? You wouldn't mind?" Carmen was shocked. We were at my house that Monday, and Carmen had just told Kyla how much she liked the shirt. "Isn't it new?" Carmen asked.

"Yeah, it's new, but I don't mind," Kyla answered with a smile. "Besides, the color will look great with your hair."

Carmen glanced over at me. I knew what she

was thinking. I had no doubt that she was remembering the time she had asked to borrow my camera. I hadn't let her because it had been brand new, and she's never let me forget it. But that's another story.

Later Carmen and I were alone in my room. I had to say something.

"Kyla's just being nice because she's new here," I said.

"So? What's wrong with that?" Carmen asked. "You act like being nice is a contagious disease or something. Some people are just like that— naturally nice."

"Well, I don't like it. It makes me look like the mean stepsister," I said. "I want *her* to be the mean stepsister. I want people to say, 'Poor Rosie, look at what she has to put up with.'"

"You're nuts," Carmen said. "Wouldn't you rather have someone nice to live with than a totally obnoxious jerk?"

"Not really," I replied. "Not when everyone likes her better than they like me."

Carmen laughed. "Well, maybe you should start being as nice as she is then."

That's when the lightbulb lit up over my head. I wasn't going to be able to make Kyla mean. But maybe I could make myself more like her. Maybe I could learn how to be . . . ugh . . . nice.

CHAPTER TWO
AN ITCHY OUTCOME

I figured that, as practice, I'd start by being nice to Timmy. Because how hard could being nice to an adorable three-year-old be? At that age, he'd be easy to please. Then I'd move on to the hard ones, like Joellen and Carmen and Kyla and Pops.

It wasn't as easy as I thought it would be. I started on Tuesday morning.

"Want to play blocks?" I asked Timmy.

"Yes!" he shouted, then ran over to me, hugged my legs, and held on. I peeled him off me, and we pulled the blocks out into the middle of the living room. The kid had enough blocks to build the Eiffel Tower. We started building towers all around us, and soon we were surrounded by a city of block buildings. The kid was pretty good at this.

When we were done, Timmy stood up. He raised his arms and hollered, "I am the king!" Then he started knocking the blocks over, laughing the whole time.

"What are you doing?" My voice went up a few octaves. "You're ruining our city!"

But it was too late. All the buildings were down and blocks were strewn all over the place. We hadn't even had time to enjoy it.

"What a dumb thing to do," I muttered.

Timmy's eyes filled with tears and drops started rolling down his cheeks. "Rosie's mad at me," he whimpered.

So much for being nice. Evidently the fun thing about playing blocks is knocking them over. I patted him on the back. Being nice was going to be harder than I thought. Time for a new plan.

By that evening, I had it all worked out. I knew Timmy liked people to read to him; he even had a favorite book about a dumb elephant. I would read the book to him, and to make it perfect, I'd throw in a bag of chocolate candies for us to share.

My father was teaching that night, Kyla was on the phone with a friend in Ohio, and Joellen was doing laundry. "Want me to read to you?" I asked Timmy.

"Yes!" he shouted, and grabbed me around the legs and held on. I peeled him off me and told him to get the book. Then I settled myself in the big chair with the bag of candy. He bounced up on my lap, shoved the book under my nose, and we began.

For every page we read, we each took a piece of candy. The story was dumb, but the candy wasn't bad.

Joellen passed through with a pile of clean laundry. She gave us a smile—a nice one, of course. Then she looked more closely, did a double take, and her eyes got huge.

"Stop!" she ordered.

Joellen dropped the clothes and grabbed the candy out of Timmy's hand. "He's allergic to chocolate," she gasped. "How much has he eaten?"

I explained to her about the one piece per page. I looked at Timmy. Sure enough, red welts were starting to appear all over his arms and face. And he was beginning to scratch.

"I want more candy," Timmy whined, and started to sniffle.

"You can have some vanilla cookies," Joellen said, "but first I want to rub some lotion on those hives and give you an antihistamine."

I gulped. "I was only trying to—"

Joellen smiled at me. "You didn't know. It's okay."

If only she weren't so nice. If only she'd yell and tell me how dumb I had been. I mean, I was trying to make the kid like me by being nice to him, but I couldn't even do that right. Instead, I had made him cry twice in one day *and* I had made him sick.

Pops didn't say anything to me when he got home. He was probably too embarrassed about having such a dumb daughter.

Joellen works in a laboratory at the hospital, but she stayed home on Wednesday to take care of Timmy. By the afternoon, he was okay. When I came home from Carmen's, he ran over, hugged my legs, and held on. I patted his head.

I told myself that I'd better stop trying to be nice to the kid before my kindness landed him in the hospital.

CHAPTER THREE
So Much for Being Neighborly

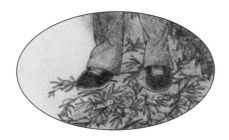

I decided that it would be better if I learned how to be nice by practicing on someone else—someone who wasn't a member of my new step-family. That way, even if I did some damage, I wouldn't have to worry about hurting my family and making them hate me.

In our neighborhood, the houses are close together. Take our house: When you go out the side door, you walk right into the neighbor's fence. The fence belongs to Jordan Fitzgerald and his grandfather.

Jordan Fitzgerald is a jerk. He's also a year older than me and ten feet taller. And he weighs at least a hundred pounds more. He can beat me in a fight. I know this because we used to average about one fight a week.

I gave up fighting with Jordan last spring,

after he gave me a fat lip and some nasty bruises. And after Pops said that if we fought again, he'd lock me in my room until I was 30.

I was glad for an excuse to stop. It wasn't much fun, getting beaten up all the time. But whenever I see Jordan now, I still can't resist saying things. Not such nice things, either. But that's another story.

Jordan lives with his grandfather. Pops says Mr. Fitzgerald isn't nearly as old as he seems. He walks all stooped over though, and he doesn't talk much. He's always out puttering in the yard, poking around at his flowers and vegetables.

On Thursday I decided to go over to Carmen's. Mr. Fitzgerald was pulling up stuff in his yard as I passed by.

"How's it going, Mr. Fitzgerald?" I called. I walked up his front path. Opportunity doesn't knock frequently, so when it does, I like to be there to answer.

Mr. Fitzgerald looked up and glared. "Don't walk on the grass," he barked.

I had my feet firmly planted on the brick walk, but I didn't point that out to him. Carmen tells me I tend to be sarcastic, so I'd have to learn to hold my tongue if I was going to be nice.

"Need some help?" I asked.

Mr. Fitzgerald looked like he was going to keel over from surprise. "I don't pay people to do work I can do myself."

Talk about grumpy. "No charge," I said, smiling. "I just thought maybe you could use some help."

He glared at me. Then he looked at the pile of green stuff at his feet. "I want to get all this planted before dark," he said. "Can't leave them out overnight. You can weed under those bushes while I plant these by the front sidewalk."

I looked over to where he was pointing. Three big bushes stood below the front windows. The pretty flowers that had been on them were gone, but the leaves were still green. Below the bushes, the ground was covered with little green sprigs.

"I can pull weeds," I told him. "I'm excellent at that. You go ahead and plant while I weed."

I sat down in front of the bushes and began to yank. Every once in a while I heard Mr. Fitzgerald grunt and groan. He was bending over, planting his flowers near the front sidewalk.

I was almost done when I heard a terrible screech.

"What are you doing?" Mr. Fitzgerald yelled.

I turned. It was me he was shouting at.

"You've ripped up the marigolds I just put in!" Mr. Fitzgerald bellowed.

I glanced at the pile of green at my feet. It sure looked like a bunch of weeds to me.

"I thought you knew what you were doing," he spat.

"I'm sorry," I whispered, scrambling to my feet. "I'll put them back."

"No, no, just get out of here!" he huffed, looking like he was about to cry. "Get out before you rip up my whole yard."

"I was just trying to be nice," I mumbled, backing away.

"Nice?" he snorted. "You're nothing but a menace."

A few minutes later I got to Carmen's house and told her what had happened.

"You meant to do the right thing," Carmen reassured me.

"Yeah . . . and he didn't have to yell," I agreed. "I've made two people cry in three days, Carm. That must be some kind of record."

"Are you giving up on your 'nice plan'?" asked Carmen.

"Of course not," I answered. "Tomorrow I'll try Joellen. I have to think of something that will really make her like me."

"You have no proof that she doesn't already like you," Carmen countered. "She's always nice to you, isn't she?"

"That's the trouble," I complained. "I'm the only one in the house who *isn't* nice. If I'm not careful, Pops will send me off to boarding school to get rid of me."

"Give me a break. He will not," Carmen said. "Now you're just sounding jealous."

"Me, jealous? Of what?"

"Of your father's new wife, and of his new stepdaughter and stepson, for starters," Carmen answered.

"I hate it when you practice psychology on me," I grumbled. "You read too many magazines."

"Maybe," said Carmen, "but it sure sounds like jealousy to me."

"I just want to fit in with them," I explained. "If I can make Joellen see how nice I can be, then I'll feel like I belong."

"In the meantime, don't try being nice to *me*," Carmen warned. "I don't want to risk it."

"What a friend," I muttered.

Then I just had to think of the ultimate nice thing to do for Joellen.

CHAPTER FOUR

LAUNDRY DISASTER

It didn't take me long to figure out what I could do for Joellen. Because she works part-time at the lab, drives Timmy back and forth from day care, and also does most of the house stuff, she's always insanely busy It was simple—I would do one of her chores, in addition to what I already did.

I already cleaned my own room and washed my own clothes. I had started doing that back when Pops and I lived alone. But I could impress Joellen and make her realize what a nice person I was by doing something more.

On Saturday Kyla took Timmy to the movies to see some dumb cartoon. I don't like cartoons; I was terrified of them as a kid. But that's another story.

Pops was on the computer. Joellen was

working at the hospital.

It wasn't hard to find the perfect thing to do. In the basement, a mountain of Joellen's clothes sat on top of the washing machine. I would do her wash. Most of the clothes were uniforms Joellen wears in the lab. A couple of what she calls "knock-around clothes" were in the pile, too. The whole thing wouldn't be more than one load. This would be a cinch.

Hot water and detergent—no sweat, I did it all the time with my own clothes. I turned the knob. The machine started to fill with water, and I dumped in the clothes and closed the cover. I'd be able to start my new mystery book while the machine did the work.

The trouble with me and mysteries is that I get really engrossed in them. My father can be talking to me and I won't even hear him. When Joellen came home, I was in Paris chasing an art thief. A few minutes later, I went into the kitchen to make myself a sandwich. Then I heard this awful groan float up from the basement. That's when I remembered the wash.

I ran downstairs. Joellen was leaning against the washing machine, supporting herself as if she was about to keel over. In her hand was a blue blouse.

"I did your wash," I said brightly. I paused,

waiting for her surprised and grateful response. I hoped it wouldn't include a hug of thanks, because I'm not good with that emotional stuff.

Joellen didn't say anything.

"I forgot to dry it," I apologized.

She turned, as if in a daze. She began pulling the rest of the clothes out of the washer. Oddly enough, they all seemed to be blue.

"You mixed colors," she practically whispered.

"It saves time," I said, not as brightly as before. "I always do all my stuff together." This wasn't the time to tell her that pretty much all my stuff is dark—reds and blues and browns and greens.

"You can't put a dark blue T-shirt in with whites," she said. "The dye runs."

I could see what she meant. Her white uniforms were now blue. Well, not all blue. On some it was just a leg, a sleeve, or part of a collar that was blue. It wouldn't have been so bad if they had turned completely blue, because then they'd be blue uniforms. But as they were, you could tell something was wrong.

Joellen was nice about the whole thing—of course. She rewashed the whites with bleach to get the blue out. The blue had affected the colors of the knock-around clothes too, but

Joellen said she didn't care about those. She said it made them look interesting.

Then she asked me (nicely) to check with her before doing her wash again. I apologized over and over, but she didn't say much to me for the rest of the day.

On Sunday I saw Carmen and told her about the laundry disaster.

"How can I make it up to Joellen?" I asked.

"Don't even try. You'll just mess things up again." Carmen always spoke her mind. She wasn't mean or anything, but she also wasn't super sweet either. That's why she was my best friend.

"Maybe I could take over the cooking," I suggested. "I used to cook all the time when it was just me and Pops."

"You microwaved frozen dinners," Carmen reminded me, "or ordered pizza. That's not cooking."

"I could try," I argued.

Carmen looked at me like I was crazy. "You'll burn the kitchen down. Leave the poor woman alone—you've done enough for her. Pick on someone else for a while."

She had a point. Maybe it was time to change direction.

CHAPTER FIVE
A PLUCKY PROBLEM

I decided to focus on Kyla next. It wasn't going to be easy, though, because we had absolutely nothing in common. She was into clothes and hairstyles and stuff like that, while I . . . well, I wasn't. But that's another story.

I was, however, smart enough to realize that asking her to play stickball with me wouldn't work. So I waited, watching and listening, for the perfect opportunity to prove just how nice I could be.

It finally arrived . . . with eyebrows—her eyebrows.

On Wednesday I was passing by the bathroom door. Kyla called to me. "Rosie, will you come look at my face for me?" She was leaning into the mirror, her nose almost touching the glass. "The light isn't very good in here.

I'm trying to figure out if my eyebrows are even. What do you think?"

I walked in, not understanding what she meant. She turned to me and put her face up close to mine. Then she pointed to her right eyebrow.

"See? I think this eyebrow goes up more than the left one," Kyla announced with a frown.

I looked. Sure enough, her right eyebrow was a little higher. And bushier.

"Yeah," I confirmed, "it does. And it's bushier, too."

"I'm going to try tweezing it," she said. She dug into the medicine chest and came out with some tweezers. "My mom does this all the time." Kyla leaned over and put her nose against the mirror. Then she went after a hair on the top of her eyebrow. But every time she pulled, nothing came out.

"Let me try," I said. What better way for me to be nice than by doing a kind sisterly thing like plucking her eyebrows for her?

We finally figured out that we couldn't do it in the bathroom, so we went into her room instead. I sat on the bed, and Kyla laid on her back and put her head in my lap. She closed her eyes, and I went to work.

It wasn't hard at all. Every time I pulled out a hair, Kyla went "ouch." But that didn't stop me. I cleared off the top of her right eyebrow. Now the left one looked a little uneven.

"I'm going to pluck a couple of hairs from the left one now," I warned.

"But there wasn't anything wrong—ouch—with the left one—ouch," Kyla said, wincing from the pain.

"Well, now it looks messy compared to the right one," I explained. "And the right one's still too bushy."

"Thanks so much—ouch—for doing this," she said. "It's really—ouch—nice of you."

I grinned. My plan was working. Just a few more from the left one . . . and one or two more from the right. You know how when you eat some icing off a cake, but then realize it's uneven? So you try to even it out by eating a little from here and then a little from there. But then before you know it, the icing's practically gone.

I won't say the eyebrows were just about gone, but they were pretty close to it. When I stopped plucking, I brushed off the pulled-out hairs with a towel. Then I studied my masterpiece.

"How does it look?" Kyla asked.

"Different," I replied after a pause.

Kyla bounced up and ran into the bathroom. I heard a faint moan. It was sort of like the sound Joellen made when she discovered the blue laundry. I walked in after Kyla. We both stared in the mirror at her eyebrows.

Kyla smiled tightly at me in the mirror. I could tell she was trying not to cry.

"It's all right," she said, her voice trembling. "They'll grow back. Not by the time school starts, but eventually. Maybe Mom will lend me her eyebrow pencil. It does look different."

"I guess I didn't do such a good job," I confessed.

"No, it's fine. I appreciate your trying," Kyla said with a weak smile. "You meant well, so thanks."

I couldn't believe it! Here I had ruined her face, possibly for life, and she was *thanking* me. I felt like a total jerk.

"I can pluck mine out, if you want," I offered. "Then we'll look the same. People will think it's a fad or something."

"I doubt your father would like that," said Kyla sadly. "We'd better just wait for mine to grow back."

That night after dinner, Pops and I had a long talk. Or rather, he had a long talk while I

had a long listen. It was all about thinking before you do something, and stuff like that. Everyone was being so nice about what I had done, even him. How was I ever going to be nice if other people kept beating me to it?

CHAPTER SIX
ROSIE FOSTER DOESN'T RUN FROM TROUBLE

On Saturday Jordan came home from summer camp, and I realized why it had been such a quiet summer so far: no dumb Jordan around to start fights and beat people up.

That afternoon I was coming back from Carmen's when I noticed Jordan sitting on the steps in front of his grandfather's house. It was too late to cross the street, and besides, Rosie Foster doesn't run from trouble.

Jordan saw me, got up, and sauntered out to the sidewalk. "Look who's here," he sneered, trying to curl his upper lip. "If it isn't Rosie, the neighborhood stinkweed."

Jordan actually thinks he's clever when he says these things.

"Hi, Jordan," I said calmly. "I see they let you out of camp early. Decided to get rid of you, did they?" I'm pretty good at dishing it out myself.

"You've been causing trouble for my grand-father," Jordan snarled. "I hear you pulled up his flowers."

I couldn't deny his accusation. "It was a mistake," I explained. "I tried to put them back, but he wouldn't let me."

"Yeah, sure," Jordan growled. "You wait for me to leave and then you harass an old man. I ought to knock you over."

That wouldn't be hard, I thought. *But at least I'd go down kicking.* Then I remembered Pops' orders: no fighting, or I'd be locked up until I was 30.

Here was the perfect chance to be nice—and to Jordan, no less! Maybe I'd have more success with him. After all, how many people were nice to him . . . ever?

"It really was a mistake," I insisted, and smiled. I tried to make it a big smile, like Joellen's and Kyla's. "You look good, Jordan. You have a nice tan. Got a chance to sit in the sun, I see."

"What do you mean?" His face tensed up. "You saying I never do anything? You saying I just sat around all summer?"

"I'm sure you did lots of things, like went swimming and played softball," I said, still smiling. "Camp can be lots of fun."

"Now you're saying I just went to have fun," he said, his voice rising. "You'd better watch it, Rosie. You're making me mad."

It doesn't take much to make Jordan mad. He's always angry about something. But that's another story.

"No, no, I'm sure you went to camp to learn things, too," I countered. My face was beginning to ache from all the smiling. "There's lots to learn at camp. And it must have been good for your grandfather to have some time to himself."

"You stinkweed!" Jordan yelled. "My grandfather didn't send me to camp to get rid of me! Now you're asking for it, Rosie. You're in big trouble!"

With that, Jordan pushed me—hard. I stopped smiling and went down backwards—also hard. And it hurt. But before getting back up, I grabbed Jordan's ankle and pulled with both hands.

He went down, too, landing on the newly planted flowers near the edge of the sidewalk. As he struggled to get up, I jumped to my feet and ran.

Even though I said before that I don't run from trouble, sometimes I do—but only when I

absolutely have to. This was one of those times.

All this just because I was trying to be nice. It wasn't my fault it didn't work. Dumb Jordan didn't deserve nice anyway. At least this time I didn't do any permanent damage or get into trouble. And as long as Pops didn't find out, hopefully it would stay that way.

CHAPTER SEVEN
KEYBOARD MALFUNCTION

Pops had said no more fighting, and since what had happened with Jordan was almost a fight, I felt guilty about it. So that night, when Pops said he had to enter some grades into the computer, I hung around. I hadn't tried being nice to him yet and figured I'd give it a shot.

"Let me help," I offered.

Pops looked at me, surprised. "Aren't there other things you'd rather do?"

"Of course not," I lied. I tried one of my sincerest smiles.

"Have you always had all those teeth?" Pops teased.

"Of course," I said, still smiling.

"Funny, I never noticed them before." Pops turned on the computer. "Okay, you read me the grades, and I'll enter them."

It only took about 15 minutes. When we'd finished, I leaned over to put Pops' papers back on the desk. My elbow accidently hit the keyboard, and a moment later I heard my father groan. It was getting to be a familiar sound.

"You just deleted everything we entered," he said softly. "I hadn't saved it yet."

So much for being nice. And this time I'd messed things up for the one person in the world who meant the most to me.

Pops patted my shoulder. "Don't worry," he reassured me. "I'll re-enter the numbers."

"I'll help." I attempted a weak smile.

"No," he said too loudly. Then his voice softened. "I'll do it myself. Thanks anyway."

He was afraid I'd mess up again.

I went to my room and sat in the middle of my bed. I thought about all my efforts at being nice: Timmy, Mr. Fitzgerald, Joellen, Kyla, Jordan, and now Pops. Six attempts, six disasters. Not one of them had worked out the way I wanted.

It was a good thing I had followed Carmen's advice and hadn't tried to be nice to her. It meant that at least I still had her for a friend.

Pops came up to my room right before I went to bed. "What's wrong, Stubby?" he asked, sitting down next to me. "You've been different lately."

I never cry. Ever. I hate to cry and pretty much refuse to do it. But that's another story.

I didn't cry this time, either. It was just my allergies acting up.

I decided to tell Pops everything. I explained my plan to become a nice person who did stuff for people, and I told him how it had backfired. When I was done, he sighed.

"So that's it," Pops said. "I knew you were acting different, but I couldn't figure out in what way. I've missed you."

Huh? I was totally confused. What did he mean he missed me? I hadn't gone anywhere.

"I love Joellen and Kyla and Timmy," he began, "and I hope someday we'll be a close family. And you're right, they're nice people. That's partially why I love them."

He looked down at his hands, which were clasped in his lap, and then continued. "Stubby, you're a rough-and-tumble sort of person. Like your mother. I like that you remind me of her."

Pops patted my shoulder. "Maybe you don't have a lot of style and grace, but that's okay. You shouldn't try to change. It's just the way you are, and there's nothing wrong with that."

I could tell what was coming, but I couldn't think of a way to prevent it. I tensed up and steeled myself against it. I tried to close my ears, but it got through anyway.

"I love you, Stubby," Pops said softly.

There. He had said it. And it wasn't as bad as I thought it would be. As a matter of fact, it felt kind of good. Maybe someday I'd even be able to say it back.

CHAPTER EIGHT
ROSIE TO THE RESCUE

On Monday afternoon, I was on my way home from Carmen's house when I walked right into trouble. Kyla and Timmy were in front of Jordan's house, and Jordan was blocking their path. His hands were on his hips, his chest was pushed out, and he had an evil grin on his face. Timmy was crying.

Jordan hadn't seen me yet, so I crossed the street and walked down part of the block. Then I crossed again and came up behind him. Jordan was too busy being a bully to even notice me.

"Hi, gang," I said casually. "What's going on?"

Jordan whirled around. When he saw it was me, he tried to sneer, but I could tell I made him nervous. "It's Rosie the stinkweed," he snarled.

"What's going on, Kyla?" I asked, looking around Jordan's big body.

Kyla was smiling, but her mouth shook a little. She was definitely scared. She clutched Timmy's hand and pulled him closer to her. "Jordan's going to charge us for walking on the sidewalk," she explained. "A dollar each time."

"It's payback for the plants you ruined," Jordan told me. He really was perfecting that sneer. He almost had it down.

"If your grandfather wants me to pay for the plants, I will," I said. "But that's between him and me. There's no way you're getting the money."

"Are you afraid I'll keep it?" he asked, his voice rising. "Are you calling me a thief?"

I stooped down, reached past Jordan, and took Timmy's free hand. "Is your mommy home, Timmy?"

He nodded. One of his tears hit my hand. I reached out and picked him up. I moved him around Jordan and then set him down in our driveway. "Go inside to your mommy, Timmy," I said. Without a word, he ran.

Kyla smiled at me, but not as nervously this time. I winked at her.

"What are we going to do about this, Jordan?" I asked. "We're not going to cross the street to avoid walking on your sidewalk. And we're not going to pay you, that's for sure."

Jordan stuck out his chest a little more. "You'll be sorry if you don't," he threatened.

I wanted to sock him right in the stomach. But Kyla was there—she wouldn't think I was nice if I hit him. Besides, Jordan had grown even bigger over the summer.

"Tell you what, Jordan," I proposed, "I'll be nice to you and offer you a deal."

"No, that's what *I'm* offering *you*," he said with a laugh. "The deal is, you pay me, and I let you go by without knocking you down."

"Well, that's not what I was thinking," I replied. "This is the deal *I'm* offering: You let us go by, and I won't tell your grandfather you broke these flowers along the sidewalk."

Jordan looked at the flowers that had been crushed when he fell on Saturday. Confusion spread across his face. "But I didn't break them!" he argued. "You pulled me down!"

"You pushed me first," I noted. "It's your fault the flowers got blitzed."

He paused for a minute while the logic of this sunk in. It finally did. "That's not fair!" he

-☼- **45**

yelled. "You can't do that—it's blackmail!"

"I guess it is." This time it was me who put my hands on my hips. Then I stuck out my chest and moved in close. I looked up at him and scowled. "Why don't you go pick on some-one your own size?" I suggested.

Jordan backed up a step. I knew I had him.

"Come on, Kyla," I said. "Let's go home."

We ran, laughing, into the kitchen. Joellen was giving Timmy oatmeal cookies. Kyla blurted out what had happened—how I had saved them both and how brilliantly I had out-witted Jordan.

Joellen gave me a big hug. It didn't feel too bad, either. Timmy grabbed my legs. Kyla winked at me. And even though Pops was at work, it still felt like there was family in the room.

⚬ ⚬ ⚬

So lately I've been thinking about all of this. Kyla really shouldn't be sharing a room with Timmy. His toys are all over the place and he goes to bed early. Maybe I'll offer her half of my room—the half without the window, of course.

And Joellen isn't too bad. She says she's going to teach me how to make oatmeal cookies. Then there's Timmy; the kid seems to like me no matter what I do to him.

I guess it's like Pops says: I may not have much style and grace, but I do okay. And if I'm not as nice as the rest of the family, well, someone's got to be tough enough to watch out for everyone. And hey, it might as well be me.